CITY OF POWER

CONNOR WHITLEY

No part of this book may be reproduced in any form or by any electronic or mechanical means. Including information storage, and retrieval systems, without written permission from the author except for the use of brief quotations in a book review.

This book is NOT legal, professional, medical, financial or any type of official advice.

Any questions about the book, rights licensing, or to contact the author, please email connorwhiteley@connorwhiteley.net

Copyright © 2023 CONNOR WHITELEY

All rights reserved.

DEDICATION
Thank you to all my readers without you I couldn't do what I love.

CHAPTER 1

Whenever I normally go to see a contact, asset or spy, I always make sure we meet in a public space with multiple escape routes and with minimal guards. That was in normal times.

These were far from normal times.

As I pulled my long black cloak and hood over my body to cover me, I made sure my swords were easy to get to and my movements were unrestricted. Because I was going to need to be free in this place, that was a certainty.

I leant against the cold wooden walls of a local pub in a large market square lined with every single shop, stall or table you could imagine. There were blacksmiths, bakers, toy makers and more all in this single little square where rows upon rows of them were.

The amazing smell of freshly baked bread mixed in with the hints of smoke that I tasted in the air, it all smelt incredible. But I wasn't here for any of those things. I was here for a simple purpose, I needed to meet someone.

People strolled around the market talking, muttering and barring at everyone else as they went around their daily business and considering how cramped the square was, I was surprised how calm everyone was.

And that concerned me. This wasn't ideal for escaping, fighting or killing in. The risk of me hurting innocent people was too high and black armoured guards were everywhere. I could see at least twenty from where I was standing.

There was the real problem. I will never deny being a female assassin is wonderful, I get to kill whoever I want for money, I get to help me and most importantly I get to be my own boss. But ever since that damn Rebellion, who wanted to kill the tyrannic Overlord, seduced me with their amazing cause wanting to free everyone, I only get to kill for them.

But their leader, Commander Coleman, is pretty sexy, hot and adorable with his amazing body and deep emerald eyes. He is a pretty boyfriend too.

A bell ringing in the middle of the square reminded me it was getting close to midday and I needed to get a move on before the typical lunch crowd came out and swarmed the market. Then escaping would be next to impossible if something went wrong.

So I made sure my long black cloak and hood were covering me and I made my way through the crowd and deep into the market.

Now by this point most people would call me paranoid, crazy or just overly cautious, well, for starters being like that keeps you alive as an assassin. And when the Overlord is your father and he's hunting you down, you tend to get very wary of spending too long in a place he controls.

Believe me, if I didn't have to be here right now, I wouldn't. I would be with the man I love but because some supernatural Hunters are, well, hunting me down and want me dead, and I found some map that I can't read. I needed to find someone who could read my map and luckily there was apparently someone here who could help me.

As I continued through the crowd, all that wonderful fresh bread and smoke smell was gone and replaced with the horrible smell of sweaty people. I really hoped this mission wasn't going to take that long.

After a few more minutes of pulling, gliding and forcing my way through the crowd, I saw a long wooden table covered in maps (that were far from accurate) and a tall woman stood there talking to a man. I didn't like her dirty black clothes that were falling apart, but I suppose I couldn't judge too much. This long black cloak was about two decades old.

I went over to the woman and watched her deal with the people in front of me.

"And that will be twenty-five coins for the Black Valley Map," she said.

The man smiled. "Oh thank you, that is just brilli! Thank you!" He gave her the money, took the map and rushed off smiling.

I went up to her. "Ever been to the Black Valley?"

The woman smiled. "Of course not Assassin, and of course the map's wrong, these people don't know any different,"

For some reason I was both impressed and extremely concerned that she knew who I was.

"Coleman tells me you're the best scholar on ancient languages outside the Capital. But judging by your maps I doubt that highly," I said coldly.

The woman laughed. "Oh Assassin, before the Overlord came to power and he killed my parents. My mother was Lady Jones Of Green Valley,"

She paused as if that was meant to mean something to me. It really didn't. I think there was a Green Valley in the far, far south of the Kingdom. Besides from that I was happily clueless about that lawless part of the Kingdom.

"The famous explorer," she said.

I just nodded.

"Assassin, I am Margret Green-Valley. Exploring, history and languages are in my blood literally. I know all of the Kingdom's history, languages and everything else. I… I just can't draw them," she said gesturing to the maps.

She wasn't lying about her inability to draw. Even I could have done a better job at this than her and according to my teachers at the Assassin Temple as a child, my drawings of men look like donkeys, and my women look like horses.

I took the journal that contained the map and opened it to the very last page to show it to her. I hated the craziness of the strange lines, ancient symbols and words that meant nothing to me. But as she looked at the map, her eyes lit up and her eyes were moving. She was reading this!

I have no idea how but she was glued to the map like it was the most fascinating thing ever.

People moaned, shouted and argued as black armoured guards pushed through the crowd. Damn it. They were on to me I needed answers now!

Margret saw the guards. "Arg! Those guards have to go. Don't have much time. The map speaks about something. A dragon's resting place. A Capital of all power. A Rod of Ultimate Sacrifice,"

I rolled my eyes. The guards were getting closer.

"Come with me," I said.

Margret stood away from her table and pulled up some of her clothes. Her legs weren't there, she was only able to walk because of two wooden sticks that had been forced in.

"A present from the Overlord," she said. "Kill him for me,"

I nodded.

"Stop!" a guard shouted.

I whipped out my swords.

Guards stormed over.

Thrusting their swords into Margret.
The guards flew at me.
I slashed my swords.
Our swords met.
I jumped into the air.
Kicking them in the heads.
People screamed in terror.
They ran out of the market.
I slashed the throat of a guard.
I ran.
Guards were too slow.
I kept running.
I dived into the chaotic crowd.
Making sure they couldn't find me.

CHAPTER 2

Commander Coleman sat on the freezing cold wood of his favourite chair inside one of his least favourite rooms in the City. It wasn't that he hated the room's so-called fine art, long oak table and chairs. It was more of what this room had come to represent in the City of Martyrs.

Even since the Rebellion had claimed, freed and defended the City Of Martyrs, so many vital decisions had been made in this room by posh snobby people who ultimately didn't know what they were talking about, so the decisions were bad and far too many lives were lost.

Coleman really wanted to never make those same mistakes as those people but as they were all dead now and the ruler of the City, Lord Castellan Richard, had named Coleman as his second-in-command, Coleman didn't have much of a choice in the matter.

Sweet oranges that tasted like the amazing bitter orange tarts he had as a child made Coleman wonder about when all this chaos would be over. He had been leading the Rebellion for a good few decades now and he just wanted it all to be over. He wanted everyone to be free, peaceful and able to enjoy life.

Coleman listened to the sounds of people being happy, laughing and cheering outside as he assumed his beautiful Assassin had returned and his people were happy to see her. He could imagine her outrage and horror at receiving the welcome now, she would hate it but she deserved it.

Coleman wasn't sure what the Assassin had wanted the map to be but for his sake and the sake of the Rebellion and Kingdom, he hoped she was in a good mood. He might not have been her boyfriend for too long but he had been it long enough to know how angry she could get!

"You okay Bossie?"

Coleman smiled as he looked at a short beautiful woman to his left with her long perfectly straight hair and leather armour. She was called Abbic and Coleman loved her as a father in a strange way, she had saved him more times than he wanted to admit and she was as strong (probably stronger) than any man he had ever met.

"Ya boss, what up?"

Coleman rolled his eyes as now he had both of his closest friends worried about him. The man to his right was Dragnist, a wonderful man, a clever man with his long beard and dirty armour.

"Relax I'm just thinking," Coleman said. Not

sure what to tell him. He just wanted his beautiful Assassin's mission to go well and hopefully she would have an answer to their Hunter problem.

Coleman had only met the Hunters once when the Assassin saved the Rebellion from extinction but they were supernatural, made from shadow and just deadly. The Assassin had fought them many more times since and just the idea of the woman he loved being killed by them was too much.

The Hunters needed to go but Coleman hated how the Overlord had trapped them and bound them to his Will using a so-called Oath Rod.

Coleman had always believed them to be myths, the stuff of legends but they were real. He wasn't sure how the magic inside the Rod made the oath between the parties unbreakable, but he never ever wanted to find out.

It still didn't make the mission any less real. The theory (which Coleman wasn't completely sure on) was to find the Oath Rod, break it and hopefully the newly freed Hunters would return to their supernatural place and leave the Kingdom alone.

Coleman wished that thinking was right but he really wasn't sure.

"Bossie?" Abbic asked.

Coleman placed a gentle hand on hers and rubbed it. "I'm okay really. I just want my Assassin back,"

Coleman felt a hard hand grab his shoulder and run down his back as someone kissed him. He raised his head, saw it was his lover and kissed the Assassin on her soft beautiful lips.

Coleman gestured her to take a seat but she shook her head. He wished she would let him hold her hand or do something more intimate than just standing next to him but he knew she would never allow that. Sadly.

"Ya mission good?" Abbic asked.

The Assassin knelt on the ground so she was in line with the table.

"What do you guys know about A Dragon's Resting Place?" she asked.

Coleman had no idea why she would be asking about a dragon. They were made up creatures, they weren't real. Coleman remembered the Assassin mentioned them a few times but he never believed they were real.

Dragnist pointed at the Assassin. "Know there were stories. Massive Stories. Dragons in Central regions,"

"What stories?" Coleman said.

"Know kiddy ones. Dragon in dead centre of Kingdom," Dragnist said to the Assassin.

Coleman looked at Abbic. She was nodding.

"Seriously Abbic? You heard the same stories?" Coleman asked.

"Yea Bossie, me heard lots of stories about Dragons. Dragons big, tasty and cuddly. One lays in the dead centre of the Kingdom. Where Capital is. I saw it,"

Coleman and the Assassin just looked at each other. "Go on,"

Abbic leant forward. "Yea Bossie and Assassin, I went there with traitorous Sis once on a mission. We went down into the sewers. Lost for hours. Found a massive chamber. Size of the City,"

Coleman really hoped his face wasn't as puzzled and doubtful as he felt.

"Then it was there. Massive skeleton of dragon, even have a dragon tooth on me," Abbic said, standing up and getting something out of her pocket.

Coleman and the Assassin looked wide-eyed at each other as Abbic threw something on the table. It was a wonderfully long tooth, easily the length of a dagger.

Dragnist picked it up. He dropped it. Licking his finger.

"What's wrong?" Coleman asked.

"Bloody thing sharp," Dragnist said.

The Assassin used a bit of her sleeve to pick it. She hissed as she put it back down. Coleman could see a part of her sleeve was sliced wide open. That tooth was sharp alright.

"How do you know this is a dragon's tooth?" Coleman asked.

The Assassin placed a hand on his shoulder. "It matches all the records and when I met the Dragons their teeth were this good. So we need to head to the capital,"

Everyone went silent.

"The map contact I met with told me three things about the map before she was killed. Something about the resting place of a dragon. A Capital of Power. A Rod of Sacrifice,"

As right as she might be, Coleman felt his stomach churn at the idea of attacking or even going anywhere near the Capital. That place would be crawling with the Overlord's guards and everything.

Coleman cocked his head when he realised it actually wouldn't be as difficult as that. When the City of Martyrs was facing annihilation and Coleman sent his message for aid out to the entire Kingdom, tens of thousands of people came to his help.

Hundreds of thousands (if not millions) had turned up since. They had the numbers to storm the capital and everyone had received basic combat training. They had an army.

A peasant army, but an army nonetheless.

Coleman stood up. "The Dragon's Resting Place, a location for the Oath Rod?"

"Yes, the Rod of Sacrifice must refer to the sacrifice the Hunters made to give up their freedom," the Assassin said.

"Bossie, we attacking Capital?"

Coleman looked at the Assassin. If she wanted to storm the Capital, kill her father and free the Kingdom he would support her, he just hoped she would love him after the battle, if he was still alive.

"Attacking Capital would be best," the Assassin said.

Coleman nodded and looked at Abbic and Dragnist. "We need a plan. But only if you two want to. I don't attack if you think it's a bad idea,"

He could feel the Assassin smile and agree with him from behind.

Abbic and Dragnist exchanged glances and started laughing. "Of course we wanna attack Bossie. We gonna kill the Overlord and free us,"

Coleman hugged the Assassin. She hugged back. Hard.

The Assassin whispered in his ear. "So we go to war my love,"

"And so the final battle begins here," Coleman said.

CHAPTER 3

Whenever I come to these meetings, I only know one thing for certain. I'll get to see the most beautiful man in the world, my stunning Coleman. The rest of the meeting tends to goes towards the slow and uninteresting end of the excitement spectrum, which is why I avoid them like the plague and I tend to go on killing missions. You know, to liven things up for myself.

Or I tend to make sure my long black cloak and hood are extra tight so I look terrifying. You wouldn't believe some of the screams I've got from scaring people like that. Good times!

But as I stood there in this rather tasteless room with its awful art and even worse oak table and chairs, I never would have expected to end up planning to invade the Capital, also known as the City of Power in the ancient language.

In all honesty I had absolutely no idea how I felt. Sure, I've wanted this from the day my bastard father threw me and my brother in the river, trying (and failing) to kill us. For as long as I could remember I've wanted to slash my swords across my father's throat, but now it was actually happening, I didn't know how I felt.

A part of me was happy, another part of me was excited and the last part was numb. I was like I didn't want this time with Coleman to end because I didn't know what he or I would do after this was all over.

My face must have spoken a thousand words as Coleman gently rubbed and kissed my hand and I looked at him and smiled.

I was about to say something when the temperature dropped. The air turned icy cold.

The Hunters appeared.

Their shadowy swords swung.

Everyone jumped to one side.

I whipped out my swords.

Charging forward.

They met my swords.

One thrusted out their hand.

Flying me across the room.

I shrieked. Whacking my head at the wall.

Coleman and the others whipped out their weapons.

They fought.

I flew over.

Jumping into the air.

Twirling my swords. Becoming a hurricane of death.

The Hunters flicked their hands. Throwing everyone else across the room.

I slashed my swords. The Hunters disappeared.

They rammed their swords into me.

I screamed in agony.

Coleman rushed over. I heard the swords. He screamed.

Warm blood splashed up my back.

Magical energy hummed.

Lightning shot across the room.

As I fell to the ground and forced myself to turn over, I stared at my beautiful Coleman who had his hands so tightly around his throat his knuckles were white. It still didn't matter too much, I could still see the blood gushing out of his wound.

I couldn't let him die. I fell forward and forced my bleeding body to crawl over to him.

White magical light in long strings wrapped around me and stopped me from moving. I couldn't allow this, I couldn't let my Coleman die alone! I wasn't going to let him die!

Then I felt the magical strings of light wrap around me and forced themselves into my back wounds. I saw Lord Castellan Richard storm into the room and my stomach churned in agony as I didn't know what was going on.

I kept wanting to fight against the strings, they might have been healing me but I had to get to Coleman. I had to be with him. I watched Richard knelt next to Coleman and Dragnist and Abbic were standing next to him blocking my view.

If I wasn't as stable as I was, I would have grabbed my swords and swung it at them only to get them away from Coleman. I had to see him. I had to see if he was okay.

Each of them exchanged concerned looks and I knew I had to do something but these damn strings kept healing me. All I could feel was a strange icy coldness cover my back.

"Strange. I was sure they would kill you," the Overlord's seductive voice said in my mind.

I rolled my eyes.

"See beautiful Daughter. We are connected now. Don't worry I cannot read your thoughts so to speak, I can only talk to you whenever I want,"

"Go away," I muttered.

"The Hunters failed me this time. They promised to kill you after their mysterious six hour disappearance in the City of Pleasure,"

I smiled at that memory. When I was freeing the City of Pleasure I was surprised that the Hunters agreed to give me six hours of freedom to try and find the object that would give them their freedom.

I know they're evil, supernatural killers but I actually felt sorry for them.

"What will you do to them?" I asked.

I heard my father laugh in my head. "Daughter, just like your mother, always a failure, a abnormal bitch of a woman, and a person who I'll enjoy killing,"

A small headache pulsed through my head as I presume the Overlord cut this strange mental connection, but another strange feeling was taking over my body. It felt familiar almost as if some strange energy was coming out of my cells.

My eyes widened as I realised this was the same sort of feeling I had in the City of Pleasure where I learnt I might share some of the same powers my mother did.

I focused back on Richard, Abbic and Dragnist as they knelt around Coleman and their faces grew paler and paler and sadder and sadder. I knew Richard with all his magical power couldn't heal Coleman, but maybe I could.

Maybe my mother gave me some kind of healing power or something. I don't know. I had to try, I wasn't going to let the man I love die without a fight.

I crawled forward and I felt the magical strings of light finish their healing work as I moved and I slapped Richard on the back.

He moved, which was good for him as I would have happily hurt him to clear the way to the man I loved. I kept crawling over to Coleman who was nothing more than a pale man covered in deep red blood and barely clinging to life.

I grabbed his leg and closed my eyes. I had no idea how this magic thing worked but back in the City of Pleasure it felt as if it came from a need, like I needed the Hunters gone and my magic allowed that to happen.

Now I needed to save my beautiful Coleman.

Slowly I felt my strange magical energy ooze into his leg and travel up into his body. It felt strange as if I was actually inside his body, feeling his wants, desires and his heart barely beating.

After a few seconds I could see out of his wound and could even see myself laying on the ground with my eyes closed. So I focused on absorbing his blood once more and closing the wound.

I opened my eyes and to my amazement, Richard, Abbic and Dragnist were staring at me like I was a crazy person. But I didn't care about them at this moment, I forced myself to my knees and grabbed Coleman's cold hands.

As I gently rubbed them I wasn't sure if he was alive or dead, he couldn't die. The Rebellion, Kingdom and most of all I needed him to lead, love and free us all. Then his eyes flickered opened and he weakly smiled.

I hugged and kissed him.

"Good job. One more person for me to kill," the Overlord echoed into my mind before leaving.

As I kissed Coleman, I knew there was only one way for me to protect my love forever. I had to kill the Overlord and I had to kill him quickly.

I was really looking forward to that!

CHAPTER 4

Commander Coleman couldn't believe what had just happened, this was all impossible. He was just on the edge of life and death, then he wasn't. It was so strange, so unnatural, so unnerving.

He had felt his beautiful, sexy Assassin inside him. He felt her moving through his body and that was just wrong, it didn't feel right in the slightest.

But at least she had saved him and Coleman was more than grateful for that, yet it was impossible that Richard who was a Lord Castellan, a god amongst men in his own right, couldn't heal him but the Assassin had.

How?

When his beautiful Assassin helped him to his feet, all Coleman wanted to do was stare into her amazing dark eyes and admire her long black cloak and hood. But he could feel Richard, Abbic and Dragnist staring at him wide eyed.

"Thank you," he said to the Assassin.

She smiled at him. "Your welcome but… but we have a problem,"

"What?" Richard asked.

The Assassin turned to face everyone. "My father can… mind talk to me now,"

Coleman and Richard started nodding.

"What Bossie? What do ya know?"

"You know the Assassin has tons of half-brother and sisters, right?" Richard asked.

Coleman held the Assassin's hands tight as he could see how uncomfortable she was becoming.

"Ya," Abbic said.

"Assassin, I hope you don't mind but I've been hunting them for years. Even before you Rebels came to the City of Martyrs whenever one came here I killed them,"

"Believe me Richard that isn't a problem," the Assassin said firmly.

Coleman couldn't believe how relieved Richard looked.

"But whenever I killed one it was like… like an echo in my mind was left of the Overlord's voice. It only lasted for a second but it was like they were talking to him seconds before they died,"

The Assassin nodded. "So… this power's from him?"

"We don't know that-" Coleman said.

"If both your mother and father had magic then it makes sense you get powers from both of them," Richard said.

Coleman just looked at Abbic and Dragnist were looked like they were watching a gripping play.

"Is it dangerous!" the Assassin shouted.

Everyone took a step back, even Coleman.

"I'm sorry," the Assassin said.

Coleman hugged her.

"No. It shouldn't be dangerous but the Hunters can come here now. This is no longer a safe place from them. I heard you found something about getting rid of them?" Richard said to the Assassin.

Coleman stood up straight. "Richard, Abbic, Dragnist, I need a full military plan for the Capital in three hours. Tell everyone to take up arms. We leave in twelve hours at first light,"

Coleman felt great. It was amazing to take charge again.

The three of them smiled and left. Coleman wasn't sure what he had just done. He wanted to invade, storm and free the Capital, but something felt wrong. It wasn't that this attack felt rushed, they had millions of potential soldiers that had all gone through basic combat training.

But this was the point his entire life had been working towards. He hoped his dad would be proud.

"And what do you want me to do?" the Assassin asked, pushing her head into his neck.

Coleman had never heard the Assassin this vulnerable, fearful or dare he say it scared. "I want you to… I want you to be safe,"

She laughed at that.

"I'm serious. The Hunters almost killed you today. I never want to lose you," Coleman said.

"I never want to lose you too, Coleman,"

"All know in all the history scriptures, the man and woman have passionate *exercise* tonight and swear their love for each other in case something bad happens,"

The Assassin playfully hit Coleman. "I don't believe in the Gods and Goddesses so I don't believe in marriage, but I would marry you Commander Coleman. And I love you from the bottom of my heart,"

Coleman felt his stomach do happy backflips at the sound of that. This cold, brutal assassin had just confessed her love for him. That was amazing, that was shocking, that was what he had always wanted.

"Whatever happens in the next few days, I will find you. In this life or the next," Coleman said.

The Assassin broke away from Coleman and closed the doors and windows to presumably make sure no one could see them.

"I don't plan on seeing you dead in the next few days," the Assassin said, loosening her long black cloak and hood. "But in case something happens to me, let's make the most of the next three hours,"

As blood rushed to wayward parts, Coleman wished these hours would never end, but he knew once they did. He would only be seeing blood, rage and death for the next few days.

And that was if he survived.

CHAPTER 5

I never wanted to leave Coleman and the rest of the Rebellion behind, but fighting on the front line was never going to be my style, my way or my purpose in finishing off the Overlord. As an assassin, I have and always will work behind enemy lines, killing a critical person here, there and everywhere.

Yet as much as I wanted to say I was simply being an assassin when I said I was leaving the Rebellion before they left, I was actually going to hunt down the dragon's resting place and try to find that Oath Rod. After almost losing the man I love, I had, I absolutely had to get rid of these Hunters.

My large black horse rode softly along the soft sand road onto the Capital as me and Abbic went, with a horrible wind making my long black cloak and hood flap in the wind. The desert that led up to the Capital was as bare as anything and a hellhole in its own right, but in the far, far distance I heard the whirling river.

I hate that river more than anything else, that damn river that almost claimed me and my brother when we were just children. I was so confused back then, I didn't know why my father had just killed my mother and was dragging us over to the river.

Yet as I felt the water drag me under, it didn't matter that I didn't understand, my survival was the only thing that mattered.

Like it does now.

As I listened to Abbic riding next to me, singing a merry little tune to herself, I was starting to really wonder why I had bought her. It was, of course, because she could lead me to the dragon's resting place, but me and her were so different.

Sure, she was a great fighter, "friend" and person, but I almost didn't want to be escorted around the Capital. For the simple reason that if my father was there, no matter how risky the shot, I was going to kill him.

A gust of hot desert breeze made me shiver for some reason and I saw that Abbic was staring at me like she had a question on her mind.

"What?" I asked.

Abbic smiled at me. "What ya gonna do when Coleman's King?"

I... I actually didn't know how to answer that. From all the conversations Coleman had had with both me and his Rebels, I had always been given the impression he was going to do a thing called democracy. I had no idea how it worked, but apparently a few decades before the Overlord came to power, that was how the Kings and rulers of the Cities were decided.

It sounded strange, problematic and just crazy to me, but I suppose after the Overlord, he needed something to happen. So why not let the people decide who they want. If they abuse their position, I'll just kill them anyway.

But given Abbic's question, she must know that and I don't know, she must be thinking that Coleman would be elected. I couldn't blame the people for wanting him as the Supreme Ruler of the Kingdom.

"I don't know. I'll be around. I'll still love him," I said coldly.

"I wanna be tha Security Chief!"

I snorted. "Ha!"

Abbic smiled too. "Just kidding, I wanna be something important,"

In the distance, I could see the very top of the massive spires of the City of Power and I felt my stomach turn, churn and flip as it finally sunk in what we were doing.

"Coleman likes you Abbic. You'll be fine, I'll make sure he gives you a good job,"

"Ta!" Abbic said with a massive smile.

As I kicked my horse a bit more, we both started to travel faster and I started to see more and more of the City of Power. The massive crystal spires that rose high into the sky and the rest of the bejewelled City shone in the desert sunlight. This wasn't going to end well, I just hoped Coleman would be okay.

"Where we heading?" Abbic asked.

I made my horse start to ride off the soft sandy road. "We need to go to one of the outer sewage drains. There's one about a mile outside the City,"

"Got ya," Abbic said.

As we both rode off deeper into the desert, the hot sun pounding on us and the sweat starting to pour down our backs. I had a terrible feeling that my father already knew what I wanted to achieve and had planned for everything.

But that didn't scare me.

It terrified me.

CHAPTER 6

Commander Coleman forced himself not to think about his beautiful Assassin, those three amazing hours were… amazing and the best three hours of his life. But Coleman was a leader, a fighter and a beacon of hope now so he had to remain focused.

As he walked along the yellow cobblestone streets of the City of Martyrs, he loved listening to the hopeful mutterings, laughter and general talking of everyone. He was a bit surprised that everyone was excited and looking forward to the attack, but he could understand.

Yet it was more than strange that when he spun round to look at the long lines of people behind him, he looked at where the old protective Wall used to be with its strong granite towers still standing, and he could have sworn one was missing. It was strange but Coleman was tired so he dismissed it and focused back on the amazing people around him.

Whilst Coleman knew the Assassin could never truly understand it, he did. Everyone in the entire Kingdom that wasn't a rich powerful person had lived for the past fifty years under a tyrant and as a slave. Coleman hated the City of Pleasure, he hated the constant fear of reaching age where the Masters or guests could grab him and use him for their entertainment. Or even worse, Coleman hated the odd Master that liked slaves a little on the young side that would grab him.

But this was everyone's chance to either free themselves and their unborn children of the tyranny, or die trying. And amazingly enough, Coleman actually didn't mind that, sure, he wanted to live, enjoy his freedom and be with the Assassin for decades to come.

Yet if he did die on the battlefield, as long as he died fighting for the freedom of his people, then he honestly didn't care.

Hints of sweat, metal and rust filled Coleman's senses as he went past a long line of blacksmiths that were producing swords, arrows and armour like there was no tomorrow. Then the scary idea of there actually being no tomorrow hit him, Coleman might have already said his goodbyes to his beautiful Assassin and wonderful Abbic, it still didn't make him feel any better.

"Commander," Richard and Dragnist said behind him.

Coleman turned around and nodded at them

both.

"We have the plans," Richard said, looking around.

Coleman gestured them to walk to him closely and in quiet voices. "What is the master plan then?"

"We storm it," Dragnist said.

Coleman had always admired Dragnist with his long beard, scar across his face and armour for his short conversations and honest opinions, on this occasion though he needed a little more.

Richard came close to Coleman's ear. "We have three million people here at last count. That's nothing to march up to the City of Power's Gate and blow it,"

Coleman cocked his head. "I remember that gate well from my dad's stories. It's two metres thick, twenty metres high at least. We don't have the explosives for it,"

"We have enough then magic can do the rest," Richard said.

That was risky. Coleman didn't know how magic worked, he didn't have magic, he didn't even know how well it could be trusted. Could he really rely on magic to save him, his Rebels and the Kingdom?

He wasn't sure and he didn't really want to find out.

"Coleman, I'm powerful enough. I can do it. I ran some tests earlier,"

Coleman's eyes widened as it dawned on him what happened to one of the granite towers that used to belong to the protective Wall around the City of

Martyrs, and what disturbed Coleman more was he realised he actually heard the collapse of the tower, but he thought him and the Assassin had broken the bed.

He was wrong!

"I see," Coleman said, still not sure.

"Don't have another option Boss," Dragnist said.

"Fine. Get a group of blacksmiths and get them to make us some shields. We'll need them the closer we get to the wall. The cart or carriage with the explosives must get to the gate," Coleman said.

As Dragnist bowed and went off to complete his orders, Coleman felt his stomach tighten as he felt as if the entire operation to free themselves of the Overlord's evil rested on one part of the plan going exactly right.

Normally Coleman liked plans to have at least some wiggle room as things always went wrong, but if those explosives weren't there or if Richard wasn't powerful enough. Then the entire mission would fail before it had even begun.

Then Coleman, Richard and three million Rebels could be sitting ducks for the Overlord to massacre.

CHAPTER 7

I slid off my large black horse and landed on the wonderfully soft sand of the desert as me and Abbic approached our destination. Ahead of us was nothing more than a little wooden shack that served as the entrance to the sewage system.

Theoretically my amazing plan is simple. Me and Abbic go into the shack, open the entrance to the sewers and go for a little walk (or swim sadly) into the City of Power. It sounded simple but considering how boiling hot it was out here, I was really hoping the sewers would be cool.

And that's how you know when an assassin finds it hot, because they actually want to go in smelly sewers! I suppose I could easily take off my long black cloak and hood but that isn't my style.

Abbic crawled up next to me and her eyes widened as the smell of sick, dust and sand attacked my senses, so I focused back on the shack and to my annoying horror, I saw five black armoured guards walking out of the shack.

Then another. Then another.

Damn it! I knew I was right about my father seeing this move, I hated it when I was predictable, I didn't want to have to fight, kill and slaughter these people so early.

But it was strange to see only seven guards, especially in black armour, so I suppose I had two choices. One, I could just wait for their black armour to heat up and they'll be forced to retreat. Or-

Abbic charged out. Roaring.

I rolled my eyes. I whipped out my swords.

I flew at the guards.

The guards were prepared.

They whipped out crossbows.

They fired.

I tackled Abbic.

We rolled into the sand.

I jumped up. Throwing my swords.

They ripped into two guards.

I charged.

Dodging the arrows.

I ripped my swords out of the corpses.

Abbic charged. She jumped on a guard. Hacking him to pieces.

I rushed over to the others.

Swinging my swords.

Slashing throats.

Shattering bones.

Blood splashed everywhere.

Within moments there were scattered pieces of seven corpses, I spat at each of them. It was ridiculous how my father had sent these people to hurt me. It was never going to work, it was cowardice that he hadn't even come, but it scared me that he would be waiting for me somewhere.

A ticking filled the air.

Abbic was about to open the shack.

I ran at her.

Tackling to the ground.

The shack exploded.

Sending deadly shards of wood everywhere.

I stood up and shook my head as I looked at each and every part of the flaming wreckage of the shack. Now that was silly, futile and pathetic, explosions weren't honourable and they were damn well cowardice.

It meant my father, the so-called grand Overlord was scared, so scared that his weak silly little daughter was coming for him. I was most certainly coming for him now and I was going to kill him.

"You alive little girl?" I heard my father asked into my mind. But the question was an honest one, he actually didn't know if I was alive or not.

I stayed silent. If I could gain an advantage over him then I was going to take it.

The Hunters appeared.

I raised my swords.

The Hunters dipped their heads and disappeared.

"Shame. It would have been nice for you to die. I

have more surprises coming my beautiful daughter, you will not reach the Dragon's resting place alive,"

I hissed as I felt him cut the mental link and I saw Abbic stare at me.

"Did he talk to ya?"

I nodded. "We have to keep moving and be careful. I don't want you to die Abbic," That sort of just came out of nowhere.

"Ah, me too Assassin. I wanna stay alive too. Be careful ya-self," Abbic said, walking off into the shack's wreckage.

I rushed over to her when she was about to pick up the sheet of metal that was covering the sewers' entrance. I took a step back and wedged one of my swords under it, using the sword as a lever in case the metal was booby trapped.

When the entrance was open, me and Abbic frowned when we saw the explosion had destroyed the ladder, there were no guards in the tunnel but the explosion had destroyed the small pathway too.

Meaning we had to go for a swim.

"Ya first,"

I rolled my eyes as I focused on the fast-flowing sewage. There were no lumps of solid debris but it was the worse colour and smell imaginable.

I took a deep foul breath.

And jumped.

CHAPTER 8

Commander Coleman rode his horse through the massive desert that led to the City of Power with one million Rebels behind him. To any other person one million might sound like overkill and a rolling death ball that was sure to kill the Overlord and defeat the City of Power.

But as much as Coleman wanted to believe that, he was hardly impressed that two million Rebels had decided to stay back at their base and Coleman hated how large the City of Power was. The Overlord easily had a million or more people behind those walls.

This was going to be far from easy but that excited Coleman a little. He wanted to get into the fight and killing the enemy.

Coleman listened to all the muttering, talking and worry behind him and he understood it all. Everyone was at least a bit concerned because no one really knew the layout or the capabilities of the Capital. Over the decades, there had been tons of rumours about horrific weapons that were capable of annihilating dragons from the stories, erasing entire armies and even turning the strongest men to ash within seconds.

Coleman didn't like any of those options but he hoped by the time the attack began, the beautiful Assassin would have finished her mission and might be able to help him, his Rebels and their master plan.

As the million people behind him went deadly silent, Coleman's mouth dropped as he started to see the tops of the massive crystal spires that the City of Power was famous for.

This was actually happening.

Worried voices and concerns started to spread throughout the Rebels behind him and Coleman just stopped. He wasn't having this, he was a leader and his leadership was needed more today than any other day in his life.

"We are here. They have probably seen us. They are probably preparing themselves to kill us!" Coleman shouted.

Everyone frowned.

"But we will fight. Because we are not fighting just for ourselves. I want to live in freedom, liberality and I want to live the life I want,"

Everyone nodded at that.

"Yet this Rebellion, this attack, everything about this is not for only us. What will do today will echo throughout history. We will be the fools that died like cowards,"

A wave of grumbling washed over the Rebels.

"Or history will remember us as heroes. Each of

us will be the brave men and women that dared to take on the Overlord. We will be remembered for millenniums to come. We will be the Saints and Demi-Gods that freed the Kingdom,"

Smiles lit up the faces of every single Rebel in front of him, and Coleman loved that.

"So my question is simple. How do you want history to remember you!"

"Victors!" everyone shouted from the top of their voice.

Coleman spun around. "Then we ride. Ride for Death. Ride for Victory. Ride For Freedom!"

Coleman kicked his horse. He charged off towards the City.

A million Rebels followed him.

The sound of two million hooves was deafening.

And that excited Coleman.

Coleman and the Overlord were going to clash and the result would determine the fate of history.

CHAPTER 9

I hate sewers!

They're disgusting, dirty and just utterly horrible. Even now as I climbed up a rusty metal ladder onto a little concrete pathway that ran along the sewers, I could still feel some disgusting mixture slipping down my leather-covered legs. I hated it!

And as for my poor long black cloak and hood, it was covered in dirt, smelly stuff so I quickly took it off and shook as much as the stuff off as I could.

But the smell was just awful and it was the worse thing I could even imagine, it was even worse than when I had hidden in a toilet to kill a target. I was more than glad after this mission, I would never have to deal with the Overlord again.

Abbic walked past me and I couldn't believe how happy she looked. She was covered in head to toe in some poo covered mixture, but she didn't even bat an eyelid (partly because she was still wiping her eyes clean). Abbic might have been an amazing person, but she was weird, but a strange loveable type of weird. (maybe I am going too soft on people now)

Both me and Abbic started walking along the small pathway and I was hoping there would be dents in the wall, loose hanging metal piping or something to grab on to, but there wasn't. I was so much concerned about falling because of a misstep, but more because this concrete hardly looked secure.

All along the path there were massive holes, cracks or chips where the concrete had fallen away. I didn't want to die before I had even reached the dragon's resting place.

"Not much further now!" Abbic shouted.

I still didn't understand why she was so happy, I was ready to kill someone, even more than usual. I had just spent hours floating, swimming and pulling myself through a range of sewer tunnels. I meant those things can bend around, separate and go into crazy patterns at a moment's notice. Believe me when I say I was happy to have Abbic with me.

But even worse! I had even been pulled under the sewage at one point!

"How much further?" I asked, trying to ignore the funny taste in my mouth.

"I donna. Maybe another few hundred metres,"

I rolled my eyes. She was meant to know exactly where this place was and-

The Hunters appeared. Someone else joined them. Their shadowy form flickered.

The Hunters disappeared.

I whipped out my swords and carefully went over to the corpse-like thing they had dropped.

It looked like a young female, wearing heavy white armour with her long brown hair, bright red skin and something around her neck. Probably a necklace.

She jumped up.

Her necklace glowed.

Throwing Abbic in the water. Holding her down.

I raised my swords.

I flew at her.

She disappeared.

I stopped.

She appeared behind me.

Putting me in a headlock.

"Now, now dear sister play nicely. Daddy wouldn't like that?" the woman said.

This was exactly what I didn't want to happen, I didn't want to run into any of my half-brothers and -sisters, and I sure as hell didn't want to run into a magical one.

"You are not my sister!" I shouted.

Abbic floated in the air. Taking a deep breath. She dropped back in.

"Do you want your friend to die?" she asked.

"I'll kill you,"

"Ha! Sister, you are not one of us anymore. The All-Father has gifted us with more powers then you possibly could imagine,"

I shook my head and my hands tensed around a

sword.

"That might be true. But I will always be the First-Born,"

I jumped back.

Knocking us over.

I flicked my sword.

Cutting her leg.

She hissed.

Her grip loosened.

I headbutted her.

She let go.

I jumped up.

Spun around.

Thrusting my blades into her chest.

I ripped off her necklace.

Throwing it against the wall. It shattered.

As Abbic popped up, I pulled her up and slapped her back as she coughed for a few minutes, taking long deep breaths as she recovered.

Whilst she coughed, I couldn't help but worry about the person I had just killed. My own half-siblings were after me now, typical Overlord always using others to do his dirty work. I might not have known how many more half-siblings I had to deal with, but at least something was now making sense.

My father make sure his so-called prized children were kept in reserve to protect him or kill the Rebellion when they got here, but now if he was sending them out to die. Then he knew for a fact what I was doing and how dangerous it was to him.

I helped Abbic up. "Please. We need to go quicker,"

Abbic smiled and started running off. "Come on then, it round tha corner. I remember now,"

With my hands tightly on my swords, I ran to keep up with her.

And I dreaded to know what was coming.

At some point I would have to face my father, and I had no idea if I could win that fight.

CHAPTER 10

Coleman flat out hated the Overlord.

As Coleman led the Rebels towards the City, he frowned at the Capital's massive brown iron walls but his focus shot towards the massive Gate. It was at least two metres thick but it was higher now, easily twenty metres high.

Two massive catapults stood firmly next to the Gate. Coleman had to get there.

He rode his horse faster and faster and faster. Sand was thrown into the air. The horse breathed heavily. Coleman's heart pounded.

This was the moment. Coleman led the Rebels this far. Now the faith of everything rested on the plan.

Bells rang out all over the City.

Black dots lined the massive City walls.

Archers fired.

Launching thousands of arrows.

Coleman kicked his horse. It shot forward.

The arrows left behind him.

Screams filled the air.

Coleman kept riding.

The Catapults were loaded.

They fired.

Massive chunks of flaming rock flew at them.

The rock was getting closer to Coleman.

Coleman forced his horse away.

They moved.

The rock smashed next to them.

The warmth licked Coleman's flesh.

He kept riding.

Rebels screamed as they were burnt.

The Archers fired again.

More arrows flew at them.

An arrow hit Coleman.

Coleman flew off his horse.

The arrow dented his armour.

His horse ran off.

The Rebels rushed past Coleman.

Hands grabbed him.

Richard threw Coleman on his horse's back.

As the Rebels used their horses to form a protective barrier around Richard, Coleman clapped his hands and all the nearby Rebels raised their massive square shields. They easily interlocked forming an unbreakable barrier around Coleman, Richard and the all important cargo.

Coleman had almost forgotten about the cargo (the explosives) that were in the wooden carriage behind them.

One shield flew away.

Then another.

Then another.

Then another.

The shields were being ripped apart.

Rebels turned to ash.

People screamed.

Flames engulfed groups of Rebels.

Coleman grabbed a shield. Waving it about. Signalling the Rebels.

Everyone broke formation.

Everyone scattered.

Everyone charged towards the Gate.

The Rebels abandoned Coleman.

Richard kept driving the carriage.

Archers fired.

Attacking the horses.

Nothing happened.

The Catapults fired.

Flaming rock zoomed towards them.

Richard tried to steer away.

The rock got closer.

Coleman threw Richard out.

He tumbled on the ground.

Coleman kicked the connection between the horses and Carriages.

It broke.

The horse ran free.

The rock was too close.

Coleman jumped.
The rock smashed into the carriage.
It exploded.
Throwing Coleman through the air.
The plan had failed.
Utterly.

CHAPTER 11

Abbic led us to a small rusty door that was built into the sewer tunnels and knelt down and started whispering something. I really hoped whatever she was doing wouldn't take too long, the horrific smell of the sewage was overwhelming. I was starting to go lightheaded.

I hated the sound of the rushing sewages behind me and I just didn't want to be in the sewers anymore. I wanted to be killing, attacking and making sure the enemy couldn't never ever hurt me, the Rebels or Coleman again.

When I saw Abbic cock her head and frown, I just wanted to kick down the door but earlier Abbic had mentioned some nonsense about needing to show respect in this place.

Rubbish!

After a few more moments, Abbic gasped and the door opened slowly. The air stunk horribly of must, mummified flesh and dust, it smelt awful but at least it was better than breathing in raw sewage.

We went through the door and flaming torches turned on revealing a rather wonderful chamber. It was beautiful in a way, brown blood splashed up against the walls. Some walls were completely covered in blood. I was sure there were paintings, symbols or something else under the blood, but I wasn't interested in that. Because in the very middle of the grand oval chamber was an immense corpse.

The dragon corpse stretched on for hundreds of metres, it was beautiful in a way. Even after so long the bright red scales were still shiny, vibrant and full of life. The only real way to tell it was an actual corpse was because of the missing eyes, tongue and missing belly, as no scales were there to protect the underbelly.

"Wow! This is awful!" Abbic shouted.

"Why? Look at all this blood, the artfulness in this blood spray is great," I said.

"Sure girly," Abbic said walking over to the dragon corpse.

As much as I wanted to explore the chamber and learn about what had happened here, I knew my beautiful sexy Coleman was probably fighting up on the surface. I had to finish this, get rid of the Hunters and go and help him. I owned him that much.

I went over to the corpse and stood in front of the head with Abbic. Even the head was beautiful and terrifying, each dagger-like tooth was twice the size of me and the head was probably ten metres tall.

"Ya know to find tha Rod?"

I took out the journal that included in the map and frowned as it had all been turned to mush by the sewage. I swore under my breath.

"The map reader said about the dragon's resting place. A city of power and something about a rod of sacrifice," I said.

"Tha City of Power must be tha City. Sacrifice?"

"What if the City of Power reference isn't talking about a City as we know it. What other dragon stories do you know?"

Abbic shrugged and tapped the dragon teeth. Her hand shot back as the teeth cut her slightly.

"Come on, you must know some?" I asked.

"Just one other. Something about tha dragon's city high in the sky and within tha hearts of dragons,"

Now that got me thinking, this chamber was an oval shape without a domed ceiling so I doubt the map is talking about a sky city, but what about a city the dragons carry about with them?

What if to them cities symbolised their togetherness, love and admiration for each other?

I took out my swords and raised them. Abbic did the same.

"Ready!" I shouted.

We swung.

Swords smashed into the teeth.

They chipped.

I heard people outside.

We swung again.

The teeth cracked.
Guards stormed in.
They charged at us.
We swung again.
The teeth shattered.
I swirled my hands. Magical energy shot out.
All the teeth shards floated up.
I through them at the guards.
Slaughtering them.
"Get inside that skull. Go to its heart. Find the Rod!" I shouted.
Three tall men walked in. Necklaces around their necks. They glowed.
Three fireballs flew towards the dragon.
I thrusted out my hand.
Stopping them.
I threw the fireballs back at them.
The fireballs disappeared.
The three men whipped out their swords.
I raised mine.
The men flew at me.
Our swords clashed.
The air hummed.
Magical energy crackled.
One man ran broke away.
The other two kicked me.
A man ran towards the dragon.
I jumped into the air.
Kicking two men back.
I shot out my hands.

White fire shot out.

Vapourising the man.

I collapsed to the ground.

My body felt weak. Broken. Pathetic.

The last two people flew at me.

Leaping into the air.

Raising their swords.

I couldn't raise mine.

I was defenceless.

The Hunters appeared.

Ripping the other men apart.

I shot up. Grabbed my swords.

Pointing them at the Hunters.

But they didn't do anything and I looked round to see Abbic kneeling on the ground with something in each hand. I put my swords away and went over to her, to see she was holding two halves of a broke Oath Rod.

I wouldn't blame anyone for thinking she was holding a broken stick made from ivory, but I knew what it was as I could strangely sense the rest of the magic pouring out of the Rod and disappearing.

That's when I started to notice Abbic's hand. They were dripping more and more blood onto the ground. Her face grew paler and paler and paler.

I looked at the Hunters. "What did you do!"

"We did nothing. Whoever freed us would die. You said it yourself a Rod of Sacrifice. She freed us. We saved you,"

This time their voices were different. Instead of

their normal shadowy voices that sounded like logs crackling on a fire, they sounded more distant, like they were speaking more thousands of miles away.

Yet I never wanted Abbic to die. I couldn't let her die for my mission. It was my duty to protect her and I failed, I couldn't-

"She knew the risks. We explained them to her. She didn't care. She didn't care about dying. She wanted to save you,"

I looked back at Abbic and stared into her lifeful, deep eyes and I knew they were telling the truth. Abbic had always been a rebel, wanting to kill the Overlord and free everyone. To her this was just her duty, something else to do in the name of the cause.

But to me. It was losing a great person, fighter and probably friend. I never wanted to lose anyone.

She moved her mouth to say something but then her corpse fell. Landing with a thud on the ground.

I gently kissed her forehead and got up, I would be back here. I would collect her body and give her a proper burial, she had sacrificed herself for me and now I had to do my part.

I watched the Hunters disappear back to their own place and I stormed out of the chamber.

The Overlord was going to pay for killing Abbic.

And he was going to know my fury!

CHAPTER 12

Coleman felt his entire world crumble around him as he watched the disgusting rubble of the carriage fall down around him. Massive chunks of flaming wood pounded the ground.

He hated all of this, this was awful disgusting and utterly disgraceful. Coleman had failed. The plan was simple enough but it all relied on that damn carriage not getting destroyed.

Now it had. Coleman didn't know what to do, he had to do something. He had to fight.

Coleman forced himself up, his hand tightly around the hilt of his sword. He was ready to fight, kill and slaughter the enemy.

But that was half the problem. All around him the million of Rebels on their horses were riding around chaotically, the immense Gate in front of him had to go. He had to destroy it.

He just didn't know how.

An arrow hit him.

Denting his armour.

Coleman smiled. He charged towards the Gate.

Other Rebels joined him. They protected Coleman.

More and more Archers fired.

Rebels fell.

Corpses hitting the ground.

Coleman kept running.

More Archers focused on them.

Coleman ran as fast as he could.

The Catapult fired.

Coleman legged it.

The flaming rocks flew at him.

Coleman jumped.

The rock smashed into Rebels.

Screams filled the air.

Coleman kept running.

Making it to the Gate.

Knowing he only had seconds, maybe a minute until guards, soldiers and whatever monsters the Overlord had, came to stop him. More like kill him. Coleman ran his hands over the cold rough metal of the Gate.

He had to find a way to open it. He couldn't let his Rebels be stuck out here and picked off one by one.

It might take the enemy hours, even days to pick off everyone. But Coleman's friends were dying and he hated that.

As his hands searched the cold rough metal for a

lock, handle or some other type of opening mechanism, he swore when he couldn't find one. He had to open the gate.

Ropes dropped down behind Coleman.

Coleman spun around.

Soldiers climbed down the ropes.

They let go.

Landing on Coleman.

They smashed their fists into him.

Pain shot through Coleman.

He hissed.

Rebels fired arrows at them.

The soldiers got off Coleman.

Coleman didn't hesitate.

He whipped out his swords.

Ramming it into their chests.

Corpses fell to the ground.

Massive torrents of fire shot out of the wall.

Coleman felt the heat against his skin. He was tens of metres away. But he still felt it.

Rebels ran. Rebels burnt. Rebels melted.

Coleman focused back on the wall. His friends were dying. He felt useless. He searched the wall.

Part of the metal melted.

Someone's hand grabbed him.

Gripping his throat.

Coleman hissed.

He swung his sword.

The sword wouldn't move.

Coleman was trapped.

He hissed.

He gagged.

He was choking.

The hand didn't let go.

Richard rushed over. Grabbed the hand. Turning it to ash.

Coleman heard screams from behind the Gate.

Coleman and Richard spun around.

Rebel corpses littered the ground. This was a disaster.

Then Coleman heard the air hum with magical energy and he looked at Richard who was smiling at him.

Richard's eyes were shooting out golden light then it shot out of his mouth too. Coleman felt as if something bad was going to happen. But Richard placed a gentle hand on his shoulders.

"Get it done, my friend. The new Lord Castellan," Richard said, as Coleman felt something slip into his body.

Coleman wanted to speak but he couldn't. He couldn't imagine losing Richard, his powerful Ruler, ally and friend. He didn't want to lose anyone but Coleman knew it was the only way.

Richard walked out into the open and stared at the Gate. Coleman carefully walked away from the Gate and stuck close to the walls, so the enemy couldn't see him.

Richard shot out his hands and started muttering ancient words. The entire world darkened, the sun was dimmed and Coleman felt his eyes strain just to see Richard.

Slowly Richard started to rise into the air and golden light shot from every single part of his body, and the air hummed, crackled and sang with magical energy. The entire battle stopped as everyone just stared at the Lord Castellan.

Then Richard flew at the Gate.

It exploded.

Shattering.

Ripping the City wide open.

Ripping out sections of the Wall.

Soldiers screamed.

Soldiers were smashed.

Soldiers died.

Richard was dead.

Coleman didn't have time to morn. The enemy was injured. The enemy was down.

Coleman raised his sword.

He charged into the City of Power.

Hundreds of thousands of Rebels followed him.

Now Coleman was one step closer to killing the Overlord.

CHAPTER 13

I loved explosions!

As I walked along the massive stone wall that went around the entire City of Power, I was forced to grab onto it as I felt a massive explosion. I hated the feeling of the wall's warm smooth surface, but I hated the soldiers even more.

In front of me for what looked like miles upon miles there were lines upon lines of black armoured soldiers all armed with swords and bows and crossbows as they prepared to smite the Rebels where they stood.

It was flat out outrageous. It was disgusting. It was why the Overlord had to die. Especially after causing the death of Abbic, I had to get revenge for her, even if it killed me.

Loud explosions, collapsing buildings and screams filled the air as I realised that explosion had annihilated the Gate and ripped massive chunks out of the protective wall around the City. I was easily a mile or two away but it was still a glorious sight.

So much death, destruction and chaos. Now that was perfect.

I pulled my long black cloak and hood tighter as I knew it was finally time for me to reveal myself. Coleman and the Rebels might be riding through the capital, but I had to draw as much as attention away from them as possible.

Granted the City of Power was beautiful in a strange way with its crystal, bejewelled houses and massive crystal spires. But these people inside the city loved their houses and spires too much.

If I wanted to get their attention all I had to do was destroy some of them.

A large chunk of rock smashed down in front of me.

I gently poked it and thankfully it wasn't too warm so I picked it up.

Below me were a few crystal houses where people were standing out with stunning knives and pots and pans. All looked beautiful but they would be utterly useless against an attacker.

I threw the rock at them.

It smashed into the house.

The crystal cracked.

It shattered.

Screams filled the streets.

People rushed out of their houses.

They were screaming as loud as they could.

Soldiers saw me.

They hesitated.
I did not.
I whipped out my swords.
Charging at them.
I jumped into the air.
Whirling around.
My blade chomped into their flesh.
Hacking their bodies apart.
I landed.
I grabbed their heads.
Throwing them hard at the houses.
The heads slammed into them.
Painting the houses red.
More people screamed in outrage.
More soldiers charged.
I slaughtered them.
I kept throwing the heads.
The crystal houses cracked.
More and more.
They collapsed.
Crossbows fired.
I spun round.
Ducking.
Soldiers were storming over to me.
I had to act.
I jumped off the Wall.
Into the City.
They kept firing.
And firing.
Arrows smashed into the crystal houses.

Crystal shards flew at me.

I kept running.

Soldiers turned a corner. Stepping out in front of me.

I ran faster.

The soldiers raised their swords.

I jumped.

Ramming my swords into their heads.

This was me. I was an Assassin.

And I was free to kill an entire City full of my enemy.

I planned to do just that.

CHAPTER 14

Coleman followed by his amazing Rebels stormed the City of Power, their swords were wet with blood, the streets ran red and the entire City was filled with the echoing screams of the Overlord's soldiers.

As Coleman passed each of the large crystal houses that lined a massive street that led right to the bottom of the crystal spires, he couldn't understand where all the soldiers were.

He had been walking down this awful street with his forces for an hour and yet after the initial slaughter, there were no enemies to be seen. Something was off.

Something was extremely wrong. And Coleman hated not knowing what was happening.

When they were close to the bottom of the crystal spires that rose like daggers into the sky, Coleman went out into a massive stone square that was easily the size of twenty football pitches and there was where the enemy was.

Hundreds upon hundreds of black armoured soldiers stormed out of the streets all around the hundreds of thousands of rebels with their swords, bows and crossbows raised.

But no one fired.

Coleman didn't know why but it surprised him when he saw twelve tall young people with glowing necklaces walk down the steps that led up to the spires. They were different skinny, slightly muscled and life filled, yet they all looked so fake. As if each one of them had been augmented so many times that they weren't even human anymore.

As Coleman focused on them more and more, he noticed that there were six men and six women, but the person walking in front and leading the others was a tall elegant woman. She wore an awfully tight white robe, black shoes and had two black swords at her waist.

Coleman knew they were just for show. The real danger was of course from the necklace. He recognised it from books. He didn't want them to use it.

"Lay down your arms," the woman said, her necklace growing bright.

No one put down their weapons. Coleman loved that.

The woman frowned and clicked her fingers. Three others' necklaces glowed. "Lay down your arms!"

Nothing again.

"You have no power here," Coleman said walking towards them.

"We are the Children of the Overlord. We have all the power. We serve him for his divine protection," they all spoke as one.

Coleman forced himself not to be shocked. These monsters couldn't be related to the Assassin, she was beautiful, sexy and adorable. These twelve were far from that.

"If you think you're so powerful then why does your father cower?" Coleman said.

"Kill him!" they all shouted. Their necklaces glowing bright white.

Coleman heard some people move, metal slashing against metal and bodies drop. He was glad he was protected but he didn't know how much longer his forces could resist their corrupting magic.

"Kill them all!" they shouted.

Coleman charged.

The Soldiers stormed towards him.

Coleman whipped out his swords.

Raising them.

The Soldiers attacked.

Swinging their swords.

Coleman ducked.

Jumped up.

Slashed their throats.

Magical energy gripped him.

Coleman dusted it off.

Soldiers punched him.
Whacking their fists into him.
Coleman fell.
The Soldiers kicked him.
Again.
And again.
Coleman leapt up.
Swinging his sword in a bloody arc.
Corpses dropped.
Fireballs flew at him.
They burnt him.
Coleman ran.
The Rebels attacked.
Swinging their weapons.
Slashing the enemy.
Blood flooded the ground.
The sound was deafening.
Ten crossbows fired.
Coleman ducked.
More soldiers stormed.
Pointing swords at his chest.
He couldn't fight alone.
The soldiers raised their swords.
They bought them down.
Someone tackled Coleman.
Knocking him away.
The Assassin kissed his cheek. Jumped up.
Flying at the enemy.
Her swords sliced the enemy.
She slashed their chests.

Magical energy filled the air.

Ice formed around them.

Coleman looked.

They were cutting him off from the Rebels.

An ice cage grew around them.

Cutting off the square from the rest of the City.

Then the twelve sisters and brothers of Coleman's beautiful Assassin fanned out into a straight line, the tall elegant woman still stood in front. She extended her hands.

Fire shot out.

The Assassin raised her hands. Her face unsure.

The fire hit it.

A torrent of white magic shot out of the Assassin.

She hissed.

More and more necklaces glowed.

More half-siblings shot out their hands.

The fire grew in intensity.

Coleman ran at them.

One of them flicked their hands.

Ice covered him.

Coleman couldn't move.

The Assassin screamed.

She sunk to her knees. She couldn't stop the torrent of fire.

She was growing weak.

She collapsed.

The fire engulfed her.

CHAPTER 15

A horrific icy coldness gripped me as the immense torrent of fire engulfed me and burned me to... death? I actually didn't know if I was dead because as I looked around nothing seemed out of place.

I was still in the City of Power with the horrible crystal spires in front of me, my awful twelve half-siblings were standing there smiling as they killed me, and the ice cage around us was standing strong.

It was honestly impressive how powerful my siblings were with their magic, but I guess it was all a part of learning. They had probably been using their magic since the day they were born, I had only been using mine for a month or less.

But the strangest thing about all of this was how cold it was, my skin felt icy and now I realised it, everyone wasn't moving. Even the massive torrent of fire that was just engulfing me, yet I could walk about.

So I went over to Coleman and saw the pain,

agony and rage in his eyes as he watched the fire engulf me. I wished I could tell him I was here, but I didn't know what I was.

Was I dead? Alive? Dying?

"Strange isn't love?" an elderly woman said.

I spun around and went to raise my swords when I realised I didn't have them. I didn't even have my long black cloak and hood. I was actually naked!

This was just embarrassing!

"Oh relax honey I've seen it all before," the woman said.

The woman seemed familiar as if I should have known her but I couldn't place her. But her strong cheekbones, long greying hair and her slim figure reminded me of someone.

"Do I know you?" I asked.

That question seemed to pain the woman, her eyes started to wet then they dried.

"I guess not. I was dead before you were thrown into the river. But I take we had a few hours before the Overlord ripped us apart,"

A memory popped into my head about me and my mother cuddling after I had just been born, she was telling me something about magic, dragons and power, and that I needed to remember something important for the future.

"You can't be my mother," I said.

My mother laughed. "Course not love, I died. I sacrificed myself. He was scared of ma power, I just planned some stuff,"

I gestured towards the torrent of fire, my siblings and Coleman. "What is all this!"

"This was always my plan. You see the True Master in the City of Pleasure as he was infecting me with his Pleasure gave ma the ability to see,"

I shook my head as I remembered that horrible creature called the True Master. It was wrong about it had sex with humans to make them his sex slaves. But somehow my mother had survived.

"Then I see ya death love. Ya would be killed by a half-sibling. So I learnt from the True Master how to infect people during sex,"

This wasn't happening. This couldn't be my mother. This was just a delusion caused by the flames killing me.

"I infected the father with a shard of my soul. It infected his body so whenever he passed on his material to another woman, it infected her. I am in each of those awful half-siblings. I am in their magic,"

My glaze hardened on her. "So when they used their magic to kill me. You could interfere,"

She nodded. "I think if I was still alive I would be proud. But time is running out. I have saved you for now but when I act, you must act. You must kill them. I love you,"

The entire world vibrated, jerked and crumbled around me.

I ran to Coleman.

The world started moving.

Coleman shrieked.

He smiled.
My Siblings screamed in rage.
They raised their hands.
Magic energy crackled around us.
White cracks appeared in the air.
Reality was breaking.
Their rage was immense.
The streets exploded.
The ice cage cracked.
The crystal spires were shattering.
They were ripping apart reality.
They thrusted out their hands.
They froze.
I had to act.
I was scared.
My siblings struggled.
They were regaining control.
I slapped Coleman. Freeing him.
We stormed over.
Whipping out our swords.
I stabbed, slashed slaughtered my siblings.
Their necklaces broke.
Their blood flooded onto the street.

And as I rammed my swords into the last two, I felt something inside my mind click. This was why the Overlord had wanted me dead, I was somehow the most powerful child he had ever had and he wanted to make sure I could never be used against him.

He failed.

And I was going to storm into those Spires. Find

him. Kill him.

    I was so close to my goal.

CITY OF POWER

CHAPTER 16

As Coleman wiped the thick coating of blood on his sword on his armour, he felt relieved that his beautiful sexy Assassin was safe. He didn't know, he didn't care, he just wanted to stay alive.

The sounds of screaming, slaughter and clashing swords filled the air and Coleman spun round. Seeing a massive army of black armoured soldiers storming into the City of Power.

He had no idea there were forces outside the City coming back to reinforce it.

Coleman looked at all the disgusting enemy corpses and the sad corpses of his friends. They were spent already, people were tired, injured and hungry.

They couldn't fight anymore. And these stupid reinforcements dared to attack and slaughter his forces. He wasn't having this!

Coleman had to hold the Rebellion together. He couldn't let it fracture. He couldn't let it die.

He just had to hold it all together long enough

for the Assassin to do her thing, kill the Overlord and free everyone.

The screams grew louder and louder as the reinforcements stormed into the City, slaughtering anyone who wasn't one of them. They didn't care about the innocent, they only cared about extermination.

That's when Coleman realised, he had to not only protect his own forces, friends, but the innocent people who supported the Overlord. It killed him inside but that was one of the things about being a leader.

Sometimes you just had to do the right thing, no matter how badly you didn't want to.

The Assassin kissed him and ran off.

Coleman watched her run into the crystal spires. He went to follow her for some reason, but the crystal around the Spires started to become thicker and impossible to break. And the crystal turned blood red.

He didn't know what the Overlord was planning but whatever he wanted with the Assassin, she had to fight it alone.

And that terrified him.

CHAPTER 17

I wanted to burn this place to the ground!

This massive oval chamber made from solid crystal looked disgusting and it was such a testament to my father's arrogance, idiocy and just him being so stupid. I would happily smash it all up.

I went over to the massive iron throne on the far side of this chamber which was clearly a throne room of some kind. And there was my father just sitting there smiling at me.

I wish I could just gut him. I hated seeing his massive seductive smile, long white robes and his long golden hair. I listened to the magical energy humming, popping and crackling in the air. This wasn't going to end well.

Then my long black cloak and hood started flapping in a wind that wasn't there. I took another step closer but froze. Bright white energy wrapped around me like ropes.

"I didn't think you would be this scared so

quickly, father,"

"Now, now daughter. You did not think at all. You haven't won,"

I wanted to cock my head but the ropes were too tight. "We have won. Your forces are dead. Your forces were weak. You have lost,"

The ropes burnt around me. I hissed.

"See daughter, you cannot do anything. Let me show you something," the Overlord said, making me float in the air as he walked over to the other side of the throne room.

"This room hasn't seen any love for years, has it?" I asked.

"I do not need the likes of Lords, my puppet Kings or anyone to help me deliver my vision,"

"Your vision? Your vision of what? Lies? Tyranny? Corruption?" I asked.

We were almost at the other side of the throne room and I watched the foggy crystal walls turned see-through and I could the raging battle below. The Rebellion was trapped. My friends were dying. I had to get free.

"See my daughter. You have not won. Your friends will die. My remaining forces will grow stronger and stronger. I will scourge the City of Martyrs from the map. You have lost,"

"You cannot do that,"

The Overlord extended his hand and aimed it at the floor. The ground crackled, hummed and vibrated as he did something. After a few moments he stopped and smiled.

"What did you do?" I asked.

"It is simple. Whatever was left in that dragon's resting place is alive once more. The Dragon lives,"

I forced myself to stop smiling as I just realised me leaving Abbic's body there might have just saved us. I was now glad I beheaded all the other bodies in the resting place.

"So what are your plans for me?"

The Overlord forced the ropes to turn me and stare at me in the eye. For the briefest of seconds I actually wondered if I was staring at a father. His eyes were soft, loving and almost caring, this might have been the kindest I had seen him in my entire life.

Then his eyes hardened. "You. You betrayed me. Your mother betrayed me. I failed to kill you once, I killed your brother, I will not fail to kill you,"

Stupid man!

I flicked my hands. The ropes burnt away. The Overlord's eyes widened.

"Witch!"

My hand shot out.

Torrents of fire roared at him.

The Overlord jumped back. Whipping out his swords.

I whipped out mine.

He flew at me.

I flew at him.

CHAPTER 18

Coleman flat out hated the Overlord.

He whipped out his swords. He raised them high in the sky. Everyone looked at him. Coleman pointed his swords at the enemy reinforcements.

Everyone charged.

The remaining hundreds of thousands flew at the enemy.

Coleman heard their rage.

The Rebels smashed into the enemy.

Coleman looked around. The crystal houses were close together.

He ran over to one. Climbing up onto the roof. He ran across the rooftops.

The enemy surged forward.

They slashed the Rebels artfully. Their movements elegant. Precise.

They kept killing.

Slicing through the Rebels like they were nothing.

Coleman ran quicker. He had to get to them.

Rebels' heads smashed.

Shattered.

Crumbled.

The enemy kept attacking.

The Rebels fell back.

Magic hummed in the air.

Crystal sealed the side streets and square.

The Rebels were trapped in the main street.

The enemy pressed their attack.

Coleman jumped into the air.

Raising his swords.

He landed.

Swinging his swords.

Slaughtering the soldiers.

The enemy grabbed him.

Pinning him against the wall.

The Rebels roared.

They marched forward.

Rushing to Coleman.

Coleman kicked the soldiers. Their grip loosened.

Coleman snapped their necks.

Flaming rocks flew through the air.

Smashing into the City.

Annihilating Crystal houses.

Innocent people screamed.

Innocent people died.

Coleman flew at the enemy. He wasn't kidding about.

His swords chomped on flesh. His kicks dented metal. He kept going.

Rebels became more savage. They charged past Coleman.

Becoming raging berserkers.

They ripped into the enemy.

Tearing out flesh.

Drinking blood.

They pressed their fingers into the enemy's eyes.

Their rage filled them.

Coleman heard something. Something strange. Something different.

The ground vibrated. Cracked. Moved.

Coleman felt something coming out of the ground. He shouted a warning.

The ground exploded. Something shot out of it.

Coleman stared at the object.

A massive blue dragon stretched its wings. It roared. Unleashing black fire.

The dragon stared at Coleman.

It zoomed towards him.

CHAPTER 19

I hated the Overlord! That bastard was going to die. My long black cloak and hood tightened around me.

The dragon roared outside.

I flew at the Overlord.

We jumped into the air.

I swung at him.

He swung at me.

Our swords clashed.

Sparkes shot out.

Thunder echoed around us.

His swords buzzed.

My swords shattered.

Deadly shards sliced my cloak.

He punched me.

He kicked me.

I landed with a thud.

The Overlord flicked his hands. Throwing me across the room.

I slammed into the crystal wall.
My head whacked it.
He flew at me.
Kicking me.
Again and again.
He kept kicking.
He slashed his sword at me.
Cutting my cheek.
My body ached.
Crippling pain filled me.
The Overlord thrusted out his hands.
Black fire charged at me.
I rolled away.
I jumped up.
Charging at him.
Fireballs shot at me.
I dodged them.
The Overlord disappeared.
I spun around.
My father tackled me.
Smashing my head into the floor.
His hands wrapped round my throat.
He squeezed.
I couldn't beat him.
His hands burnt hot.
I screamed.
My neck burned.
My lungs burned.
Everything was burnt.
He kept squeezing.

I struggled. I kicked. I punched.

He was too strong.

The air moved.

A sword swung at the Overlord.

He ducked.

Jumping off me.

Abbic stood there. She was alive. She was strong.

She threw me a sword.

The entire spire shook.

The Dragon smashed into the spire.

Massive flaming rocks smashed too.

The Overlord cursed.

As the spires shook more and more as the massive flaming rocks smashed into it, I knew this was the end. The Rebellion would survive and-

Abbic screamed as the Overlord thrusted his swords into her. Turning her body to ash.

How dare he! She had saved me, protected me, given me a second chance. This wasn't on!

I roared.

I flew at the Overlord.

He disappeared.

Reappearing by the crystal wall.

I charged at him.

Thrusting out my hands.

Torrents of fire shot out.

The Overlord hissed.

I kept running.

I kept charging.

I tackled the Overlord.

Pushing him against the crystal wall.
The wall cracked.
It collapsed.
I gripped him.
We flew out of the Spire.
Plumping towards the ground.
The Overlord screamed.
I gripped his throat.
Torrents of fire pouring out of my hands.
He screamed.
He tried to escape.
He couldn't.
He wasn't strong enough.
I was. I was an Assassin.
I grabbed a knife off his own belt.
I slashed it across his throat.
He smiled. He bled. He died.
More fire shot out of my hands.
Annihilating his body.
I was so close to the ground.
I almost wanted to hit it.

But as I waved my hands I felt magical energy circle me and create a cushion between me and the ground so I landed gracefully.

My father was dead. Abbic was dead. So many good people were dead.

A dragon roared.
Immense fire roared out of its mouth.
Catapults were fired.
Smashing into the dragon.

Rebels burnt.

Rebels died.

Rebels were slaughtered.

The dragon kept attacking.

It kept killing.

I saw Coleman. He was in trouble. The Dragon had him.

The Dragon was going to eat him.

I ran.

I ran towards them.

I swirled my hands.

Shattered crystal floated up.

The entire crystal Spires broke away from the ground.

I whistled.

The dragon stared at me. It smiled. It dropped Coleman.

It opened its mouth. Fire was about to pour out.

I thrusted out my hands.

As all the crystal shards and the entire crystal spires shot into the dragon, it screamed in utter agony. It threw the crystal shards, Spires and dragon so hard that they would all crash outside the City of Power.

Dead.

I ran over to Coleman.

But thankfully he just laid there on the ground smiling at me, he was happy to be alive (hell I was happy he was alive), yet I sort of knew he was more happy to see me, and that I was okay.

And as I looked around taking in all the death, destruction and chaos the City was in, I actually had to admit that I was okay. The Overlord was defeated, the Rebellion was safe and my beautiful Coleman was safe too.

But my glaze turned back to Coleman, I knew there was something else that had to be done first, before everything was truly over.

There had to be a coronation and I had to know my future.

CHAPTER 20
Two Weeks Later

Coleman took long deep breathes of the crisp clean air of the City of Martyrs after his coronation speech and he walked off the large wooden stage and stood in the archway of a little shop. He didn't know what shop it was, but that didn't matter.

Coleman couldn't believe that everything was truly over, and an immense wave of pleasure, excitement and happiness was washed over him. He had led a Rebellion, almost destroyed it and then rebuilt into the unstoppable force that had conquered the Capital.

Of course Coleman knew that everyone else had been a major part. His amazing Rebels that had been with him from the start, the brilliant three million people who had left the slavery (and safety) of their homes to him, and his amazing sexy Assassin.

Without her none of this could be possible, so Coleman had made his speech where the millions of people all over the Kingdom had voted him in as their new King. But what truly surprised Coleman even more than him actually being ruler, was that every single man and woman over the age of 18 had come out to vote.

Not a single person didn't vote.

And even more surprisingly, only one man didn't vote for Coleman, but he was exiled by his friends, City and the entire Kingdom. Coleman didn't want that but he had to respect the wishes of his people.

As Coleman stood there and listened to the cheering, laughing and happiness of everyone as the parties started, wonderful plates of food were bought out and bands started playing. Coleman just stood there amazed that this was all happening.

Sure it had happened two or three months ago after the City of Martyrs was freed, but what delighted Coleman was that this was happening all over the Kingdom. Every single City, village and town was partying, celebrating and wishing the future was as bright as they dreamed.

In all honesty it wouldn't be hard for Coleman to dazzle these people, anything would have been better than the decades of the Overlord's rule. But Coleman still wanted, needed to do his subjects proud. He would serve each and every one of them and make sure they would be proud to have voted for him.

And maybe he'll get in again in five years' time.

The air smelt amazing of fresh sweet fruit, rich pies and so many more amazing sweet and savoury flavours that Coleman didn't want to wait to find out what everyone had cooked up.

Coleman started walking through the City of Martyrs, smiling and waving to anyone he saw. Apparently these were pockets of Overlord soldiers scattered throughout the Kingdom, but after rewarding Dragnist with the title of Lord Commander, he had dispatched him to kill them all.

As a new ruler it may have made sense to arrest them, put them on trial then kill them. But Coleman didn't need votes to know that everyone just wanted to move on and look to the future, and Coleman was no fool. The longer those Overlord soldiers were alive, the more time the Overlord's ideology had to spread, corrupt and lead to a new force that would enslave the Kingdom once more.

Coleman wasn't going to let that happen.

Coleman shook some people's hands, thanked them for their help and started to walk over to the horses. His beautiful Assassin had left this morning for a town about two hours ride away, she wanted him to join her and Coleman wanted to join her.

He had no idea why she wanted him to go somewhere else, but a tiny part of Coleman just wanted them to have some private time. Time where they weren't leaders, freedom fighters and now King and King's Consort.

He just wanted them to be a man and woman deeply in love.

So Coleman took another look around and

couldn't stop himself from smiling. This was all amazing, he had done what no one thought he could do. He had freed millions of people from a tyrant so they could live a life they wanted, how they wanted.

Sure he might never get into power again, but Coleman didn't care. He never wanted power, he wanted Richard to take over the ruling part of the Kingdom. All because Coleman had done his part, he had freed everyone.

And that was more than enough to him.

CHAPTER 21

Sometimes I honestly shock myself, I wasn't surprised so much by the fact that Coleman had gotten elected, or that the election had taken place, but I was actually amazed at how pleased I was. I couldn't be happier for Coleman, the Kingdom and even myself.

I was no longer just an Assassin with the evil Overlord as my father, I was something more. I was loved, cared about and I was a hero.

I wasn't sure if I wanted to be a hero, I was just doing my job but for some reason, I knew that was a lie. If my job was just to kill the Overlord, I would have done that years ago. But my job as an Assassin, a female assassin at that, is to kill the guilty and protect the innocent.

And if I had killed my father years ago then someone else would have just taken his place and punished the innocent for killing him. Simply because I was so good at killing they never would have known it was me.

With the sound of music, laughing and happiness filling my ears, I stared down the massive street. I stared at amazement at all the dishes of fine sausage rolls, crispy golden lamb and succulent juicy pork. And thousands of the other dishes.

The air smelt amazing with hints of thyme, rosemary and chilly. Crisp meat, juicy bacon and sweet fruit. The entire town was an amazing explosion of wonderful smells, tastes and colour.

But there was a reason why I was here. I didn't just come to a random town, I came to the town where it all began. Sure the large wooden houses were different and they were painted in the blood of the Overlord's soldiers that these people had killed.

Yet the massive stone wall with raising towers was still there. I remember running towards them, fighting on them and releasing the birds. All in an effort to get my message about the Overlord's invasion to Coleman. That simple message had started it all. I had come here to try and save the Rebellion when the Overlord launched an attack out of the City of Death.

It all seemed so strange now and even though it was only a few months ago, it felt like a lifetime ago.

The music stopped as everyone sank to their knees for a few seconds before my beautiful Coleman ordered them to stand, party and keep celebrating. Then he said this was their victory as much as his.

I actually agreed with him, before I joined the

Rebellion properly, I really thought I could do it all on my own. I thought I could kill the Overlord, free everyone and keep being an Assassin.

But now I was something more, something better. I had found my family, not a family of blood, but a family of love and brotherhood. A family I would happily die for (technically did) but I wasn't going anywhere.

I would like to think (and I do know) that my beautiful little brother who the Overlord killed when he attacked the Assassin Temple would be proud of me. I knew he would be but I wished he was here, my sweet little brother was amazing, he was the only blood family I had left, and he was dead. It killed me when that happened.

But he would be proud that I overcame my assassin training and learnt to love again and find a family.

I would be Coleman's King Consort, probably marry him because it's tradition and I would serve by his side for all the years we remained in power. Because like him, governing the Kingdom was only part of the mission now, the real mission that no one would ever see would be to stop another Overlord from rising and wanting to turn the Kingdom back to the *good old ways*.

It sounded ridiculous and when Coleman first mentioned it to me, I didn't believe him. I couldn't understand how someone might want to turn the Kingdom back into the corrupted, tyrannical and slave state that it had been. But as Coleman pointed out, people always tell themselves that the old ways were better if the current ways were lacking.

I agreed.

So my mission was to protect everyone, stop another Overlord rising and kill any dangers to our freedom.

I felt Coleman wrap his strong arms around me and he started to kiss my neck. I couldn't help my smile because this was what I had always wanted but never allowed myself to think about it. I had always wanted a man to love me, care for me and want to be with me.

And now I had one.

I turned around and kissed Coleman's soft sexy lips. Hard. And as we kept kissing, I knew the future was going to be bright. Because there were no more threats to everything, the entire Kingdom could celebrate, love each other and live without fear.

As me and Coleman walked hand in hand and spoke to our people, I just smiled at him, because I truly did love him.

And I know my life was going to be amazing.

Just as I always wanted.

AUTHOR'S NOTE
Thank you for reading, I hope you enjoyed it.

Like in all my other Author's Note in my books, I wanted to quickly tell you about some of the inspiration behind this book. Therefore, for the City of Power book, I knew I wanted to do the final book based on the Capital, but the problem with that was to keep with the titles of the series. I had to give the Capital a City name so hence the map reading and the Capital being called the City of Power.

Then the book became a part of tying everything together. Like exploring more about the Hunters, the history of the Assassin and the half-siblings that the Assassin has. As well as this was really the last chance for us to explore the Assassin's mother and what happened to her as her storyline had been revealed in major ways in City of Pleasure.

So it had all had to happen in this book and the main inspiration behind this was a strange mixture of the last Hunger Games book, because the entire thing was based on attacking the Capital (even though I haven't read that book in years) and another series that I stopped reading but liked the titles, and I can't remember the series now for the life of me.

Overall, I hope you really enjoyed the book and please check out the rest of my fantasy, science fiction and other books on my website or at your favourite book retailer.

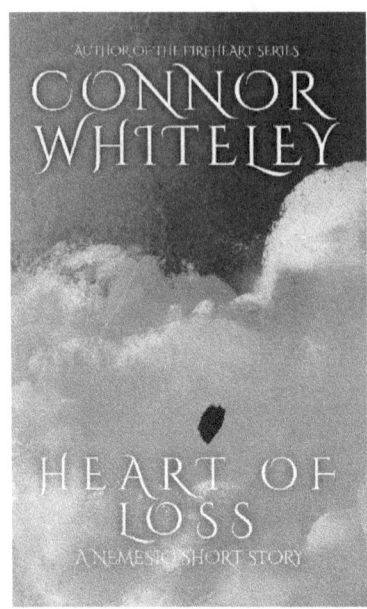

GET YOUR FREE AND EXCLUSIVE SHORT STORY NOW! LEARN ABOUT NEMESIO'S PAST!

https://www.subscribepage.com/fireheart

Keep up to date with exclusive deals on Connor Whiteley's Books, as well as the latest news about new releases and so much more!

Sign up for the Grab a Book and Chill Monthly newsletter, and you'll get one **FREE** ebook just for signing up: Agents of The Emperor Collection.

Sign Up Now!

https://dl.bookfunnel.com/f4p5xkprbk

About the author:

Connor Whiteley is the author of over 60 books in the sci-fi fantasy, nonfiction psychology and books for writer's genre and he is a Human Branding Speaker and Consultant.

He is a passionate warhammer 40,000 reader, psychology student and author.

Who narrates his own audiobooks and he hosts The Psychology World Podcast.

All whilst studying Psychology at the University of Kent, England.

Also, he was a former Explorer Scout where he gave a speech to the Maltese President in August 2018 and he attended Prince Charles' 70th Birthday Party at Buckingham Palace in May 2018.

Plus, he is a self-confessed coffee lover!

OTHER SHORT STORIES BY CONNOR WHITELEY

Blade of The Emperor
Arbiter's Truth
The Bloodied Rose
Asmodia's Wrath
Heart of A Killer
Emissary of Blood
Computation of Battle
Old One's Wrath
Puppets and Masters
Ship of Plague
Interrogation
Edge of Failure
One Way Choice
Acceptable Losses
Balance of Power
Good Idea At The Time
Escape Plan
Escape In The Hesitation
Inspiration In Need
Singing Warriors
Dragon Coins
Dragon Tea
Dragon Rider
Knowledge is Power
Killer of Polluters

Climate of Death
Sacrifice of the Soul
Heart of The Flesheater
Heart of The Regent
Heart of The Standing
Feline of The Lost
Heart of The Story
The Family Mailing Affair
Defining Criminality
The Martian Affair
A Cheating Affair
The Little Café Affair
Mountain of Death
Prisoner's Fight
Claws of Death
Bitter Air
Honey Hunt
Blade On A Train
City of Fire
Awaiting Death
Poison In The Candy Cane
Christmas Innocence
You Better Watch Out
Christmas Theft
Trouble In Christmas
Smell of The Lake
Problem In A Car

Theft, Past and Team
Embezzler In The Room
A Strange Way To Go
A Horrible Way To Go
Ann Awful Way To Go
An Old Way To Go
A Fishy Way To Go
A Pointy Way To Go
A High Way To Go
A Fiery Way To Go
A Glassy Way To Go
A Chocolatey Way To Go
Kendra Detective Mystery Collection Volume 1
Kendra Detective Mystery Collection Volume 2
Stealing A Chance At Freedom
Glassblowing and Death
Theft of Independence
Cookie Thief
Marble Thief
Book Thief
Art Thief

Other books by Connor Whiteley:

The Fireheart Fantasy Series
Heart of Fire
Heart of Lies
Heart of Prophecy
Heart of Bones
Heart of Fate

City of Assassins (Urban Fantasy)
City of Death
City of Marytrs
City of Pleasure
City of Power

Agents of The Emperor
Return of The Ancient Ones
Vigilance
Angels of Fire

The Garro Series- Fantasy/Sci-fi
GARRO: GALAXY'S END
GARRO: RISE OF THE ORDER
GARRO: END TIMES
GARRO: SHORT STORIES
GARRO: COLLECTION
GARRO: HERESY

GARRO: FAITHLESS
GARRO: DESTROYER OF WORLDS
GARRO: COLLECTIONS BOOK 4-6
GARRO: MISTRESS OF BLOOD
GARRO: BEACON OF HOPE
GARRO: END OF DAYS

Winter Series- Fantasy Trilogy Books
WINTER'S COMING
WINTER'S HUNT
WINTER'S REVENGE
WINTER'S DISSENSION

Bettie English Private Eye Series
A Very Private Woman
The Russian Case

Miscellaneous:
RETURN
FREEDOM
SALVATION
Reflection of Mount Flame
The Masked One
The Great Deer

All books in 'An Introductory Series':
BIOLOGICAL PSYCHOLOGY 3RD EDITION
COGNITIVE PSYCHOLOGY THIRD EDITION
SOCIAL PSYCHOLOGY- 3RD EDITION
ABNORMAL PSYCHOLOGY 3RD EDITION
PSYCHOLOGY OF RELATIONSHIPS- 3RD EDITION
DEVELOPMENTAL PSYCHOLOGY 3RD EDITION
HEALTH PSYCHOLOGY
RESEARCH IN PSYCHOLOGY
A GUIDE TO MENTAL HEALTH AND TREATMENT AROUND THE WORLD- A GLOBAL LOOK AT DEPRESSION
FORENSIC PSYCHOLOGY
THE FORENSIC PSYCHOLOGY OF THEFT, BURGLARY AND OTHER CRIMES AGAINST PROPERTY
CRIMINAL PROFILING: A FORENSIC PSYCHOLOGY GUIDE TO FBI PROFILING AND GEOGRAPHICAL AND STATISTICAL PROFILING.
CLINICAL PSYCHOLOGY
FORMULATION IN PSYCHOTHERAPY

CITY OF POWER

PERSONALITY PSYCHOLOGY AND INDIVIDUAL DIFFERENCES
CLINICAL PSYCHOLOGY REFLECTIONS VOLUME 1
CLINICAL PSYCHOLOGY REFLECTIONS VOLUME 2
CULT PSYCHOLOGY
Police Psychology

www.ingramcontent.com/pod-product-compliance
Lightning Source LLC
LaVergne TN
LVHW011845060526
838200LV00054B/4165